HAZEL THE GUINEA PIG

*Hazel was a brown, sleek, beautiful guinea pig
with eyes as glossy and black as raisins.*

HAZEL
THE
GUINEA PIG

by
A. N. WILSON

illustrated by
JONATHAN HEALE

CANDLEWICK PRESS
CAMBRIDGE, MASSACHUSETTS

Text copyright © 1989 by A. N. Wilson
Illustrations copyright © 1989 by Jonathan Heale

First U. S. edition 1992
First published in Great Britain in 1989 by
Walker Books Ltd., London.

Library of Congress Cataloging-in-Publication Data

Wilson, A. N., 1950-
Hazel the guinea pig / A. N. Wilson ; illustrated by Jonathan Heale.
—1st U. S. ed.

Originally published: London : Walker Books, 1989.
Summary: Hazel the guinea pig gets stuck in a boot, sees her
hutch invaded by an enemy guinea pig, and gives birth
unexpectedly.
ISBN 1-56402-013-4
[1. Guinea pigs—Fiction.]   I. Heale. Jonathan, ill.   II. Title.
PZ7.W686Haz   1992
[Fic]—dc20   91-71850

10 9 8 7 6 5 4 3 2
Printed in the United States

Candlewick Press
2067 Massachusetts Avenue
Cambridge, Massachusetts 02140

CONTENTS

*To be honest, Hazel was a very
fat guinea pig indeed.*

HAZEL'S SEARCH

Hazel was a brown, sleek, beautiful guinea pig with eyes as glossy and black as raisins. Like most guinea pigs, Hazel enjoyed her food. She was far from slender. To be honest, Hazel was a very fat guinea pig indeed. In fact, she was so fat that she looked as though she had been blown up like a balloon. Her cheeks bulged. Her glossy black eyes seemed to pop out of her ample face. And her body was a sphere, a ball of glossy brown fur.

But Hazel was an extremely handsome creature. It suited her to be fat, just as it suits some *people* to be fat. And fat is what she was.

Hazel liked to explore. When she was in her hutch, she sometimes ran from one room to the next, as though she were looking for some-

thing. Life in two rooms becomes more interesting if it can be turned into an everlasting
quest. She waddled into her living room and
ate some food. Then she nuzzled around behind the food bowl, as if she were looking for
something there. Then she ran back into her
bedroom and burrowed into the hay, as
though she had lost something—something
very precious.

When her young owner took her out of the
hutch, Hazel liked to explore some more.

"No," she seemed to say, turning this way
and that on someone's lap. "It's not here.
Let's try up there." And she would scuttle up
under someone's sweater.

"Hazel loves going up your sweater," said
one of the children one afternoon, when their
mother was out shopping.

"Yes, she does," agreed the other child.
"She likes to explore."

"I suppose I do," thought Hazel. "I like to

10

explore. I wonder what there is down *this* dark passage. I'll just have a look. You never know."

When she went down that dark passage, Hazel felt wool pressing hard against her cheeks, and she heard the girl's voice crying out, "Hazel! What are you doing?"

"She is going up your sweater," said the boy's voice.

Hazel tried to advance farther into the sleeve-tunnel, but it was tight and dark and woolly. Before long, she could feel the girl pulling at her hind legs and dragging her back into the daylight.

Hazel wriggled and struggled to be free. She had begun to feel a little hungry, and she would not have refused if someone had offered her a piece of bread or a carrot. (These were her favorite foods.)

She found that the girl had put her down on the kitchen floor, and she was able to run around freely. Here there was much to explore.

"Worth a look," thought Hazel, as she scuttled to the other end of the kitchen and peered between the bars of the fireplace screen. A fire was glowing beyond the bars, and Hazel wondered whether she might have a closer look at it. Very bright, fire is. Very interesting. On the other hand, it is also. . . . Hazel wondered how she would describe it. Well, *hot* would be one word. The bars of the screen almost hurt her nose even before she had started to sniff them.

"I remember now," she thought. "Fire's hot. Ah well, now that I've had a look at that, it is time to search around for . . . for . . ."

What was it that Hazel was always searching for and seeking?

She ran along the baseboard and listened at a mouse hole. All was quiet within, for this was a household with cats. There was no mouse making merry there.

Hazel peered at the bottom of a cabinet, but the door was shut.

And then, at the other end of the kitchen, she saw another door. This time it was an open door.

No one was taking as much notice of her as they should have when Hazel, very swift, though very fat on her short legs, made her rapid progress toward the open door. She ran! Oh, how Hazel ran! She ran out of the kitchen and into the tiled hall, through the legs of a chair, and up to a most interesting selection of articles lying higgledy-piggledy by the back door.

"Now," Hazel asked herself, "what have we here?"

She had stopped feeling slightly hungry. She had become famished. And she had decided that there was no point in waiting for someone to give her a stalk or a leaf, a carrot or a crust. She should go and look for it. That's what she should do.

Hazel's mind had wandered by the time she reached the heap of interesting articles. She had forgotten exactly what it was that she had decided. Explore, that was it. But what for?

Now then, what had she here? Hazel paused. At that moment, she looked as round and as brown and as sleek and as fat as she had ever looked in her life. Just ahead of her nose, she had seen a rain boot resting on its side.

"Well," said Hazel to herself, "if that isn't a tunnel! What was it that I had decided to go and do? *Explore*! That was it. Well, where better to explore than in a tunnel? And my being hungry and all, who knows? Like as not, there's a carrot or a piece of bread at the end of that . . . yes, that tunnel. *Tunnel*'s the word for it."

And with great eagerness, Hazel advanced

Just ahead of her nose, she had
seen a rain boot. . . .

into the boot. Inside it smelled sort of rubbery, but she pressed on, fearless, toward the toe.

"Now this," she thought, "is what I'd call dark. Very, very dark, this tunnel. Dark and . . ."—she added to herself as she got farther and farther inside the boot—"dark and, well, *narrow* would be one word for it. Yes, I would most definitely say that this tunnel was narrow. Still, what was it? Carrots and crusts?"

By now Hazel was in complete darkness, and she realized two very disagreeable facts. One was that the sides of the tunnel were narrower than her own fat little body. Another sad fact was that though her feet were still scampering and scuttling, she had stopped moving.

In short, Hazel was stuck.

She had never walked backward in her life. She had only walked forward. And the more she scampered and scuttled with her sharp little claws, the more stuck Hazel became. The sides of the rain boot pressed against her fur. She had become a prisoner.

In the kitchen the children had noticed Hazel's absence, but they were unable to explain it.

"Hazel!" called the girl's voice. "Hazel, where are you?"

"You should have looked where she was going," said the boy's voice.

"It wasn't my fault," said the girl, whose voice had become a little quavery. "Hazel! Hazel, darling! Where *are* you?"

The little girl, who was nearly eight (tomorrow would be her birthday), had begun a frantic search for her beloved guinea pig at one end of the kitchen. Her older brother, aged ten, sat and watched.

The girl looked behind the fireplace screen.

"Hazel!" called the girl's voice.
"Hazel, where are you?"

Hazel could surely not have gotten into the fire? She looked at the mouse hole in the baseboard. Hazel could surely not have gotten through that! She looked behind the sofa. She even looked in the cabinet. But Hazel was nowhere to be seen.

"I bet she fell in the fire," said the boy unpleasantly. "She's probably burned up by now. Mom shouldn't let you keep a guinea pig if you can't take care of it."

"What about your hamster, then?"

"That was different, and besides, I was only six. I took *care* of Hammy. It wasn't my fault he escaped. You can't take care of Hazel."

"I can."

"Why are you crying, then?"

"I'm not . . ." *crying*, his sister tried to say. But by the end of her sentence, she was.

Hazel did not have an opinion about whether the girl was crying. She only wished that they could get her out of the tunnel. She let out agonized squeaks to inform the children of her predicament.

The little girl, through her sobs, came out into the hall and heard Hazel squeaking. But she could not tell where Hazel was hidden.

"Hazel!" she called again. "Where are you?"

But what could a guinea pig *do*? She could not say the words: "I am in a tunnel. *Stuck* would be the word for it." She could only squeal, and when this had no effect, she was once more silent.

"I heard her. I really heard her out here," said the girl.

"You're making such a noise yourself, how could you hear her?" her brother asked impatiently.

"She was squealing," said the girl.

"I can't see her," said the boy.

Hazel heard him kick the hall chair and scrape its legs on the tiles. The children were looking underneath the chair. Then they opened the closet under the stairs and called Hazel's name. They had no idea that she was just under their noses, stuck in the rain boot.

Inside the boot it was still very dark. It also felt hot, and Hazel was beginning to find it difficult to breathe. There was another strange thing. The longer she stayed in the narrow tunnel, the narrower it seemed. She felt the sides of the boot grow tighter and tighter against her sides. Surely she was not getting fatter inside the boot? By now she was ravenously hungry, and she could not remember when she had last seen a decent cabbage stalk or a bowl of bran. It was a sorry state that Hazel had gotten herself into, and the thought of it made her start squealing again. This time she was not squealing to alert the children. She was just squealing in despair.

"I heard her that time," said the boy. "You don't suppose she's gotten underneath that pile of boots and shoes by the back door?"

No sooner had these words been spoken than Hazel felt the tunnel heaving and shaking and shuddering.

Thump!

Something had fallen on top of the tunnel.

Bang!

To the right and left of her, boots, shoes, roller skates, sneakers, tennis balls, and rubber flip-flops were being thrown.

And then Hazel got the feeling you get in a fairground if ever you are brave and silly enough to go on the roller coaster. Her stomach heaved and jumped. And although she was still squeezed tightly in the blackness of the tunnel, she felt the tunnel being lifted into the air.

"She's in the boot!" the boy cried aloud from the back door.

"Where? Where? Give her to me!" shouted his sister.

"Don't be rough."

"I'm not being rough."

"You are."

"Give her to me," said the girl.

While these words were being exchanged, Hazel could feel the tunnel swaying in the air and being dragged to and fro. And then she heard the girl say, "We'll put you on the kitchen table, Hazel dear, and we will have you out in a jiffy."

"A jiffy, eh?" thought Hazel. "Well, I'd rather be in a jiffy than in a tunnel. Just as long as it isn't what I would call a *narrow* jiffy."

But before she had time to ask herself what a jiffy *was*, Hazel was screaming in violent agony and terror. The girl's hand had reached inside the boot and was pulling Hazel by her hind legs. It felt as if her legs were being pulled off. However much the girl pulled at the back, the front part of Hazel's body still remained stuck in the boot. And the more the girl pulled, the more Hazel screamed and the more she wanted to get away from the pain by burrowing deeper and deeper into the toe of the boot.

"You're hurting her," said the boy.

"I'm trying to get her out. Come on, Hazel."

And once more, the girl thrust her hand into the boot in an attempt to extricate the captive.

But Hazel was stuck. She was more stuck than ever. And by now her screams could be heard half a mile away. She sounded like a big farmyard pig just about to be made into bacon.

"Let me try," said the boy.

But the boy's hand was bigger than his sister's, and he was afraid to grab Hazel in case he would squash her altogether. He tried, as gently as he could, to hold the boot upside-down and to shake Hazel out. Her screams did not grow any quieter.

"There is only one thing to do," said the girl. "We will have to cut the boot with scissors, the way some babies are born."

"Mom will go crazy if you cut my boot," said the boy.

"But Hazel is *stuck*," said the girl.

Hazel, very much stuck, stopped screaming for a moment and listened. She heard one of the children opening a drawer. She heard the rattle of metal objects. Then the boot began to heave and to shake once more, and the children were once more quarreling.

"It's my boot."

"She's my guinea pig."

"You'll jab her if you wave those scissors like that."

"I will not."

"I forbid you to cut my boot."

"Too bad."

"Either you give me those scissors and let

me cut the boot, or Hazel will stay in the boot and die. Oh, stop *blubbering*."

Hazel was silent. She was dumb with terror. The tunnel had started to shake again, and at her back she could hear the noise of scissor blades, coming closer and closer and closer. Snip! Snip! Snip!

"I'll have to cut the boot all the way up."

"Well, make sure you don't cut Hazel."

"I'll feel it when the scissors go anywhere near her body," said the boy.

"You mean, *she'll* feel it," said the girl.

Hazel could indeed feel it. She could feel the cold steel of the blade creeping up the hot, fat side of her body. And as soon as the scissors touched her, she screamed again.

"You've stabbed her!"

"Yikes!"

"You've stabbed her!"

"Of course I haven't."

But the boy did not sound very sure. His

scissors *had* come very close to the guinea pig, and he could not be sure whether or not he had accidentally nicked her with the blade.

But, in fact, Hazel was all right. Suddenly she saw daylight. The walls of the tunnel were ripped away. A hand was clasping her firmly and gently and giving her to the girl.

"Here you are. No cuts. She's safe."

What a relief! What a drama!

In a few minutes Hazel found herself sitting on the girl's lap nibbling a cauliflower stalk. It was very consoling to be free again, and I am sorry to say that in the excitement of the moment, Hazel went to the bathroom on the girl's dress.

"Never mind, Hazel. This is not the dress I am wearing for my birthday party tomorrow. Do you know what Mom is giving me for my birthday, Hazel? She says it's a surprise. But now that you are safe and well, I can't imagine a nicer present than you, dear Hazel; just you,

*Suddenly Hazel saw daylight. The walls
of the tunnel were ripped away.*

safe and well again after your adventure."

Well, an adventure was one thing you could call it. Hazel was not sure, but she thought you could easily call it an adventure. As for birthday presents, she did not know about those. At the moment, she was finding the cauliflower stalk most sustaining. When she had eaten enough, she burrowed once more into the girl's sweater. Now, what *was* it she had been looking for when she first set out to explore and got stuck in that horrible tunnel?

Coming back into the kitchen a few minutes later, the boy said, "I've put the boot in an old plastic bag and hidden it in the trash can. The trash collectors come tomorrow."

"And tomorrow is my birthday!" said his sister. She was happy now. All her tears were dry.

"I don't know what I'm supposed to wear the next time it rains," said the boy. "But it is true that those boots were getting tight for me and one of them leaked. Mom keeps saying she'll get me some new ones, but she never remembers."

Just then they heard the squawk and squeak of their mother's bicycle brakes. Looking through the window, the boy saw his mother leaning her bicycle against the far wall at the end of the garden and hurrying into the shed where Hazel's hutch was kept.

"Mom's back," said the boy. "Here she is, coming down the garden path. And it looks as though she has a package for your birthday."

"Is that my birthday present, Mom?" asked the girl when their mother came indoors and placed a large bag on the kitchen table.

"Your birthday present is a surprise," said Mom. "This bag is some more boots for your brother. He said that the old ones fit, but that they were getting tight." And out of her bag she produced a lovely pair of black, shiny boots, as black and as shiny as Hazel's eyes.

"Thanks, Mom," said the boy. "You're right, my old boots were getting tight."

"They shouldn't leave them lying around," Hazel thought. "Not if they are tight, and a girl might feel inclined to go exploring up them. No wonder I got stuck if they were tight. Tight is what they felt."

The new boots, apparently, were a perfect fit. While the boy tried them on and expressed his pleasure in them, Mom talked to Hazel and the girl.

"Here you sit, Hazel," said Mom, "and I have been bicycling around town, buying boots and I don't know what. You have a lucky life."

"Well," said the girl, but her brother shot her a glance that made it clear that she should not tell Mom the story of how Hazel got stuck in the boot, and how they had to cut her out of it with kitchen scissors.

"Is it a dull life for you, Hazel?" asked Mom, stroking the back of the guinea pig's head. "All on your own, with nothing to do?"

"I don't think it's dull," said the girl.

"I think it's a *little* dull," said Mom. "You can't really imagine a guinea pig having an adventure, can you? She just has her food, and she scampers around and . . . oh, look what she's done on your dress! Come on, Hazel, back in the hutch before you do any more damage."

"My dress is drying now," said the girl.

"I'll put her back in the hutch just the same," said Mom.

"*I* will," said the girl.

"No," said Mom, "you stay here. *I* will put Hazel back in the hutch."

Mom went to the fridge and came back with two carrots and two pieces of bread.

"Mom!" said the girl. "Hazel's fat enough as it is. She'll burst if she eats all that."

*"Oh, look what she's done
on your dress!"*

"She might get hungry," said Mom.

"Quite right," thought Hazel. "You never know when you might get what I call hungry."

"Come on, Hazel," said Mom. And Hazel, who by now had recovered from the secret adventure of the boot, was very happy when Mom picked her up and carried her off down the garden path.

Mom opened the door of the hutch very carefully with one hand and put inside it the two carrots and the two pieces of bread.

"Carrots," thought Hazel. "Now I must remember to look for those. I'll have a look in the living room, and then—if there's what I'd call time, I'll run over and have a look in the bedroom. Worth a look."

"Now, Hazel," said Mom. "In you go."

And Mom put Hazel safely back inside the hutch.

First Hazel looked at her bowl of dried food, and then she ran into the bedroom to peep at the hay on her bedroom floor. Then she scuttled back into the living room to look for the bread and carrots. And then she paused. Had she really seen what she thought she had seen in the bedroom? She thought that she had seen a handsome black, white, and orange boy guinea pig, the color of tobacco.

She turned. She chirruped. That *was* what she had seen! She went back into the bedroom and burrowed in the hay.

The new guinea pig was called Tobacco.
They made a very happy pair.

THE VISIT OF FUDGE

The new guinea pig was called Tobacco. He had a contented nature, he enjoyed his food, and he liked Hazel. They made a very happy pair. Hazel lost that slight wistfulness which she had had when she lived on her own. She no longer scurried around so much, everlastingly on the lookout for something. She had found what she was looking for. She discovered that many of life's simple pleasures were twice as enjoyable when they were shared with an amiable companion. In the old days, if someone had put an apple core into the hutch, she would have eaten it cheerfully enough. But now, as well as there being something to eat there was something to talk about.

"Anything important?" Tobacco called

from the bedroom, hearing that there had been a delivery next door.

"Some fruit, by the looks of things," said Hazel.

"Fruit, eh?"

Hazel never fully remembered *all* the fruits that there were, but Tobacco had a real knowledge of the subject. As he came out of the bedroom he said, "It could be a piece of orange peel. Then again, it could be a pear."

"Ar," said Hazel. "It could be a pear."

She was eating some of it and couldn't rightly make up her mind.

"It could be, girl," Tobacco conceded.

He had taken to calling Hazel "girl," and she seemed to like it, though she never called him "boy."

"But as it happens, this is . . ."

"It's nice," said Hazel.

"That it is," said Tobacco, sinking his teeth into the apple core. He had momentarily forgotten what this particular fruit was called, but it was very delicious.

When they had nibbled it down to almost nothing, Tobacco shared with Hazel some of his almost-memories of the old days. He had no memory for things that had happened very recently. But there were some fascinating things lodged in his memory from three or four weeks before, when he lived with his parents in a rather overcrowded hutch. He did not *know* that they were his parents, and when he thought of his father, it was simply a half memory of an old black and white guinea pig who had talked a lot.

"I knew a guinea pig once," said Tobacco, remembering his father but not knowing that it was his father.

"Now I can't remember whether I ever did," said Hazel.

"This guinea pig," said Tobacco, "he said the best fruit to eat was called Barn Anna.

White, I believe it is."

"More like a cabbage?" asked Hazel.

"Could be."

"This fruit was nice," said Hazel, surveying the few remnants of an apple core. "What did you say it was? My memory's terrible. Not like yours."

Tobacco went to the bars of the hutch and sniffed.

"It's a really nice day today, girl. Let's hope they put us out on the lawn."

"Oh, that would be nice," said Hazel. "I like the lawn."

A few minutes later the children came and put the guinea pigs in the run on the lawn. When Tobacco and Hazel ran around together on the grass, they were a joy to see. They were so happy, so playful, so carefree.

Now it so happened that on that day, the children who took care of the guinea pigs were planning a surprise for Tobacco. The girl had told all her school friends about him. Yes, Hazel was a wonderful, beautiful creature. And when she had owned just Hazel, the girl had believed that it would not have been possible to love a guinea pig more. But after Tobacco arrived, well . . . comparisons are odious. The girl did love Tobacco very, very much indeed. He was so friendly and happy, and he chirruped when you picked him up and put him in your sweater. The girl had told her friends that Tobacco was the handsomest, the most chirruping, the friendliest, and the best *boy* guinea pig in the world.

The girl's best friend, another girl called Rona, was also very fond of guinea pigs, and she had one whom she considered the prettiest, the most chirruping, etc.: Fudge was a special breed known by guinea pig experts as American Crested.

The girl who took care of Hazel and Tobacco knew that no girl guinea pig could be nicer than Hazel. But she agreed with Rona that it would be very exciting if Fudge could have some babies. And if the prettiest, most chirruping, et cetera, were to mate with the handsomest, most chirruping, et cetera, they would have the most et cetera *baby* guinea pigs in the world. Some of them might even turn out to be et cetera *cresteds*, and that was an exciting thought. So the girl had agreed that Rona should bring Fudge that Saturday morning, and that Fudge should spend the weekend in a separate hutch with Tobacco. But as with so many things that sound like a good idea, it actually turned out badly.

"This," Tobacco was saying, "is what I'd call juicy. Really juicy grass, this."

Hazel gazed at him admiringly. He had such a way of putting things. But just then the side of the run was lifted up, and a hand reached in and grabbed Tobacco in midsentence. He was just saying, "I knew this guinea pig once who knew about grass—"

"Don't squeak, Baccy darling," said the girl. "You are going to meet Fudge."

"Oh, he *is* sweet," said Rona. "He's so nice and glossy."

"Fudge is nice, too," said the girl politely.

Tobacco stayed still in the girl's hands and quieted down. She sat on the grass and held him in her lap. He looked this way and that. This way he could see his wife, running around the run, saying, "Ah, juicy, that's the word for it." And that way, the other way, he could see some knees, clad in a pair of jeans, and some hands on which the nails were bitten down, and in the hands the silliest-looking guinea pig Tobacco had ever seen in his life. It was an orange affair (not that he troubled himself about colors; as it happened he couldn't make out colors). And it had this sort of fur-hat thing on its head. Well, really! Tobacco tried to think of a word for it and selected the word *silly*.

"I mean," he said quietly to himself, "a head's a head. Just a head. You don't need to go dolling it up with a sort of *hat* effort."

"I think he chirruped then," said the girl optimistically.

"It sounded more like a whimper," said her friend Rona.

"No," said the girl firmly, "it was a definite chirrup."

"I so very much hope," said Rona, "that they'll like one another."

"It is impossible not to like Tobacco," said the girl.

"Shall we try putting them together in the hutch?" said Rona.

The girl stood up and carried Tobacco down to the garden shed where the hutches were, and Rona followed carrying Fudge. The girl opened the bedroom door of the hutch and put Tobacco inside. Tobacco felt disap-

*It was the silliest-looking guinea pig
Tobacco had ever seen in his life.*

pointed that he had been given such a very short time in the run. He had been enjoying the fresh air, and the grass, and the good talk. But he contented himself with the certainty that Hazel would soon be brought to join him.

"Shall we put Fudge in the bedroom, too?" asked the girl.

"No," said Rona, "I'll put her in this living room part of the hutch."

So this they did. And then they shut the doors, making sure that they were fastened securely. The two girls peered into the hutch. Fudge chirruped and nuzzled into Tobacco's feeding bowl.

"She loves that bran," said Rona. Then she added coyly, "I guess they want to be left alone."

And the two girls walked out of the shed, leaving the guinea pigs to their own devices. They went and sat on the lawn and watched Hazel munching her grass feast in the run.

"Wouldn't it be lovely if Fudge had some babies?" said Rona.

"A whole litter of crested Tobaccos," said her friend. "As glossy and friendly and sweet as Tobacco, only with little crests on their heads! If Fudge *does* have a litter of babies, would you let me have one?"

"Would your mom let you have three guinea pigs?" asked Rona.

"Of course she wouldn't," said the girl's brother, who had come out to join them. He thought it was wimpy to be drooling over the little creatures in this way. He wanted someone to play tennis with and waved a racket grandly. "Come and play a game."

"Not if you're going to be rude about Baccy," said his sister.

"I'd like to play," said Rona.

So they all went to the nearby park to play tennis.

Inside the hutch, Tobacco lay in his hay

bed for a while and felt sad. Then he decided that there was no point in sulking, and he had no sooner made this sensible decision than his spirits lifted. He heard some munching and scuffling next door in the living room, and he happily assumed that Hazel had been brought to join him.

"I could have used more time on the grass, girl," he called from the bedroom. But as he waddled out to join her, he did not hear the familiar cries of "Ar" or "That's right." Instead, to his absolute amazement, he saw Silly Hat bold as brass, standing in *their* living room and eating *their* food.

"Get back in there if you value your life," said Fudge angrily.

"What did you say?"

"You heard."

"That's not polite," said Tobacco. "And who are you, I would like to know."

As he spoke, all the fur stood up on his

48

back. He felt a violent hostility to Silly Hat. He felt so angry that he would have liked to bite the silly pig.

"Warned you!" said Fudge, who ran toward Tobacco with fur on edge and teeth bared.

The fight was sharp and furious. Fudge tried to jump on Tobacco's back and bite his neck. Tobacco threw Fudge off and scratched at the enemy with his claws. Then to his great satisfaction, he managed to get a good mouthful of Fudge's crest. He yanked and tugged with his teeth and succeeded in pulling out some of the fur before Fudge hit him with a claw on the side of his head and knocked him dizzy.

"I'll teach you to pull my crown, you little brat!" howled Fudge.

"Crown! Huh! Silly hat is more like it," said Tobacco.

He regretted saying this, because it excited

Then to his great satisfaction, Tobacco managed to get a good mouthful of Fudge's crest.

in Fudge a truly murderous fury.

"No one insults the cresteds and gets away with it," hissed Fudge through two slightly protruberant front teeth, both very sharp. "Particularly not a thing like you."

Fudge pounced on poor Tobacco and knocked him over on his back. Tobacco waved his paws and shrieked in despair; he was completely powerless. He looked up and saw the open mouth of Fudge and two long sharp fangs coming closer and closer to his throat.

Then, just in the nick of time, the door of the hutch opened, and Mom's hand reached inside and picked up Tobacco. He was quivering with fright, and he had a cut on the side of his head.

"Poor Tobacco," said Mom.

She stroked him, kissed him, and examined his cut. It was not as bad as it looked. Mom put Tobacco in the run with Hazel. Then

*The door of the hutch opened, and Mom's hand
reached inside and picked up Tobacco.*

Mom went to the garden shed once more. She took Fudge out of Tobacco and Hazel's hutch.

"Come on, Fudge," said Mom. "We'll put you in this spare hutch over here."

It just happened that Mom had been weeding the flower bed near the garden shed. She had heard the furious squeakings of Fudge and Tobacco and had gone to see what was the matter with them. Mom did not blame either of the guinea pigs for fighting. She was not angry with Fudge for having flown at Tobacco. She realized that it was just nature. She was just a *little* angry with the children for having left the guinea pigs before checking that they were getting along well. A nasty incident had been narrowly avoided.

In the run Tobacco was still shaking with the shock of it all.

"How have you gone and gotten that nasty cut?" asked Hazel, her mouth full of grass.

"Silly Hat did it," said Tobacco.

"What's that then?"

"You've been all right, girl, eating grass in here."

"Ah," agreed Hazel. "I've been all right."

"But they've gone and bought this terrible pig with a thing on its head like you've never seen."

"What kind of a thing?"

"Well, *hat*'s the only word for it," said Tobacco. "And a darned silly one at that."

"Watch your language," said Hazel.

"Well, silly, then, and never mind about the darned."

"That's better."

"And where do you think they've gone and put this Silly Hat creature?"

"Where?"

"In our hutch, that's where."

"What, not in *our* hutch."

"That's right, girl."

"Another guinea pig?"

54

"Like I says, with this darned—sorry—with this Silly Hat thing on its head."

"That wouldn't be right," said Hazel. "Not on its head, a hat."

And then Tobacco felt fonder of Hazel than he had ever felt before, and he went and stood so that his nose was very nearly touching her nose. And then he thought how beautiful she was—so plump and sleek and brown and glossy. And he made a noise that the girl called chirruping—but actually he was saying, "That's my girl."

They talked for ages about Silly Hat while they munched their grass. Tobacco talked so much about it partly because he couldn't stop, and partly to remind himself of what had happened in case he forgot it.

"Then it came at me," he said.

"Oh *dear*," said Hazel.

"But I gave it all I've got," said Tobacco.

"I bet you did," said Hazel, "but you

shouldn't go fighting."

Although Hazel said this, she was secretly very proud of Tobacco for defending their hutch against an intruder.

Tobacco said, "Then I says, 'Don't come a step further,' I says, 'or I won't be actionable for my answers.' "

"Oh *dear!*" exclaimed Hazel.

"It came at me," said Tobacco, "but I was ready. Its teeth were bared, and it was hissing and oh, girl—the stink of the creature."

"What did you do?" asked Hazel.

"Do?" asked Tobacco. "What else could I do? I just fought it. I gave as good as I got, girl."

"I'm sure," said Hazel. "But you shouldn't have gotten into a fight."

"It came at me," said Tobacco, "but I knocked it sideways. Flat. That's what I knocked it. I really think if that lady hadn't come along, Silly Hat would have been a goner."

"I'm glad you didn't . . ." Hazel hesitated. Either she could not find the word "kill," or she did not want to use it. Instead she asked, "Where are we going to live? We can't share a hutch with Silly Hat."

"We shall *protest*," said Tobacco. "If they pick us up and try to put us in that hutch with Silly Hat, we must wriggle, we must struggle, we must shout. We must never allow them to put us in there."

When the children returned from their game and tried to catch Tobacco and Hazel, they found it astonishingly difficult. Both the guinea pigs ran around the run and wouldn't be caught. And when they were eventually caught, they squealed and squealed, demanding to be free. But it was all right. When they got back to their hutch they found that Silly Hat had been taken away. She had gone home with Rona.

"I can still smell that *thing* in here, you

"Surely you've realized by now," said
Mom, "that Fudge is a boy."

know, girl," said Tobacco, indignantly walking up and down the living room.

"Oh come to bed and stop worrying."

Much later, as they lay in the hay, Tobacco said quietly to Hazel, "I'm glad it's gone."

"Me too," said Hazel.

"I'm glad it's just you and me, girl."

"That's right," said Hazel.

The whole incident caused the children embarrassment and worry. The girl had told Rona that Tobacco was so friendly. Rona had said the same about Fudge.

"And it would have been so wonderful if Fudge could have had Tobacco's babies," said the girl.

"Wonderful, indeed," said Mom. "It would have been a miracle."

"Why is that?" asked the girl.

"Surely you've realized by now," said Mom, "that Fudge is a boy."

After a few weeks of living with Tobacco,
Hazel became even fatter.

BROWN 'UN

Hazel was a very fat guinea pig. After a few weeks of living with Tobacco, however, she became even fatter. The children began to suspect that she was eating too much.

"It's like Mom and Dad," said the boy. "If Mom is on her own, she just eats a stick of celery and a tub of cottage cheese for her lunch. But when Dad's at home, she cooks a leg of lamb, roast potatoes, vegetables, and cake."

"Sometimes," said the girl. "Not always. Sometimes it's stew and dumplings, followed by rhubarb pie or—"

"I know, I know," said the boy. "That was just an example, stupid. Married people eat more than single people, it's a well-known fact."

"How do *you* know?" asked his sister.

The boy did not bother to answer this question. He just said, "It's the same with guinea pigs."

"But Hazel doesn't give Tobacco his food," said the girl. "I'm the one who puts out the dried food and the raw carrots and the—"

"When you remember," said the boy. "Usually it's Mom who feeds them."

"It is not," said the girl. "Anyway, you may be right. I will try giving them less to eat in the future."

So that day she only half filled the guinea pigs' bowl with bran and instead of giving them one raw carrot each, she cut a carrot in two and put that in their cage.

Hazel and Tobacco did not notice that their rations had been halved when the food arrived.

"Grub's up," squeaked Tobacco.

"Eh?"

"Wonder what it'll be today. Now I feel like a nice carrot."

"Carrots? Oh good."

And Hazel scuttled into the living room part of their cage and started to nibble her half carrot. She found her meal very delicious. But when she had eaten her carrot and rummaged around in the blue plastic food bowl, she felt her meal had been strangely unsustaining. Tobacco felt the same.

"I'll be glad when we're out on the lawn," said Hazel.

"Same here," said Tobacco. "I could just do with a few mouthfuls of grass. Just to round off the meal nicely."

But that day it was raining, and the children did not put the guinea pigs out in the run. After about an hour and a half they were squeaking with hunger.

This went on for two or three days. The little girl gave the guinea pigs smaller meals, and they both felt acutely hungry and miserable. And there was this curious fact. In spite of her special diet, Hazel remained decidedly stout. In fact, the less she ate, the fatter she became.

Then the girl had a horrible thought. She had several times seen films and pictures of very hungry people in Africa, and she remembered that when poor children are dying of starvation, their stomachs swell up. Perhaps the reason that Hazel was getting fatter and fatter was that she was starving.

"Don't be stupid," said her brother. "How can she be starving? And anyway, that doesn't explain why she is *so* much fatter than Tobacco."

So they decided to ask Mom why Hazel was getting so fat, but Mom just smiled and said, "Wait and see."

Mom also told the girl to go on feeding Hazel and Tobacco a normal amount of food.

She also said that it would be better, even though the sun was now shining, if Hazel did not go out in the run. Tobacco could go in the run but not Hazel.

"I think you can guess why Hazel wants to be a little quieter," said Mom.

"She doesn't like the hot weather," said the boy. "That's why."

But the girl had by now guessed the real reason that Hazel had become so very, very fat. She took special care to clean out the hutch every day. She made sure that Hazel had plenty of clean hay in the bedroom. And she gave her extra little bowls of bread and milk to eat.

"It's not just herself that she has to feed, is it, Mom?" said the girl. But the boy just looked puzzled. And sure enough, after not many days, the girl's expectations were fulfilled.

It happened early one morning before the people in the house were up. Tobacco and

Hazel were in the hutch. It was a bright sunny morning and outside the birds were singing. Tobacco had woken early, thinking of his breakfast.

"Hazel," he said, "if someone were to come along and offer me a cabbage stalk, I shouldn't say no."

"I should," said Hazel.

Early in the morning, a guinea pig does not always listen to what his wife is saying, so Tobacco continued, "Or a nice piece of lettuce. I shouldn't say no to a nice piece of lettuce."

"Don't feel like eating," said Hazel.

"What's that?"

"It's all right," said Hazel. "Just don't feel like my food, that's all."

"Are you all right, girl?" asked Tobacco, suddenly anxious for Hazel's welfare.

"Oh, I'm all *right*," said Hazel. "Just got a *twinge*, that's all."

"A twinge, eh? What sort of a twinge? A twinge of hunger?"

"More like just a twinge," said Hazel. "A twinge inside, like."

"You'll be better when you've got a drop of grub inside you," said Tobacco.

"All the same," said Hazel, "think I'll just go into the bedroom and lie down in the hay."

An hour later Mom brought Tobacco his breakfast, and after she had put some bran in his bowl and some lettuce leaves on the living room floor, she opened the bedroom door and peered into the hay. Then Mom called, "Children! Children! Come and see!"

Tobacco had been thinking that his wife was being a long time in the bedroom. He wondered what all the excitement was about, and between mouthfuls of a really delicious piece of lettuce he called through, "Everything all right, dear?"

"I think so," Hazel called back.

*And there he saw Hazel and three bedraggled
little guinea pigs beside her.*

"Grub's up," said Tobacco.

But Hazel did not come. So Tobacco pushed his nose into the bedroom. And there he saw Hazel and three bedraggled little guinea pigs lying beside her in the hay.

"Now how did *those* get in there?" was Tobacco's first thought. And then he realized what had happened. He knew why Hazel was so quiet that morning. He stared at the mystery of it. Half an hour before, Hazel had just been an overweight guinea pig. And now— here were three *new* guinea pigs. He knew where they had come from, but even so it felt like magic. And the magic feeling made him both sad and happy at once.

By then Mom and the little girl were opening the bedroom door and peering inside.

"Don't touch them," said Mom. "Just look."

"Oh, look!" said the girl. "She's going to feed them."

The little guinea pigs, who still looked rather bedraggled and surprised to be existing at all, were beginning to cluster around their mother for some milk.

"Are you all right, dear?" asked Tobacco.

"Yes," said Hazel.

"Oh listen, they're *squeaking*," said the girl.

"Squeaking or speaking," said Mom.

And then, instead of feeding the babies all at once, Hazel lay down and . . . had another baby!

It was a very small baby, not much bigger than a mouse, and for a while it lay perfectly still. Mom and the little girl and Tobacco all watched, and they all feared the worst. But the baby was not dead. Hazel was a good mother. She cleaned it up, and she licked it, and she petted it, and soon the tiny, mouselike little guinea pig was staggering around with the others.

"That all?" asked Tobacco. Naturally he

was proud and pleased to be a father, but enough is enough.

"I *think* so," said Hazel.

And before long the four babies had all been suckled and were lying contentedly against their mother's soft, furry body.

There was no room for all six of them in one hutch. Mom insisted that Tobacco be moved into a separate hutch, which made him very desolate and lonely. His hutch was at a right angle to Hazel's, so they could see each other through the wire. Every morning he would call out, "All right, girl?" And Hazel would reply, "Right you are." Each evening Tobacco would say, "Sleep well, girl!" and Hazel would say, "Right you are." But all through the day and night, he was lonely without her. She was not so lonely without him. She had four other guinea pigs for company and found it an exhausting occupation keeping them fed and trying to teach them some manners.

The guinea pigs themselves did not know about Mom's decree. Mom had decreed that two guinea pigs were enough, and rather meanly, Dad and the boy had agreed with her. It had been further decreed that when the guinea pigs were four weeks old, they should be taken to the pet shop. This was only sensible.

"So you must not get too fond of them," said Mom to the little girl. "There really is no point."

Of course there is a point in getting fond of anything. It was easy to say that they should not get fond of the guinea pigs. But if you saw them every day, as the little girl did, you couldn't *help* getting fond of them.

So it was agreed that the babies of Hazel and Tobacco should be called One, Two, Three, and Four. "One" was a saucy, rather brash guinea pig, nearly all white with a few brown patches on his back. He was the first who started to eat solids, and he strutted around the cage as if he owned it. "Two" was a tortoiseshell and white male, slightly more mysterious in character. He was very fond of his food and kept himself to himself.

"Three" was an amiably stupid brown and white female who very early on took to imitating her mother's phrases. But she never knew the meaning of them. If Hazel called, "Come and have some milk!" "Three" would rush into the bedroom saying, "That would be right." If Hazel licked "Three" behind the ears and said, "Why can't you be *neat?*" "Three" would answer, "Right you are." And when she was settling down to sleep in the hay, very sleepy with her eyes shut, "Three" sometimes murmured, "I wouldn't mind a nice run on the lawn."

So much for the guinea pigs known as "One," "Two," and "Three."

But "Four" was the little girl's favorite. She liked "Four" because she was small and brown and vulnerable. She liked "Four" because she chirruped when you picked her up. She liked "Four" because she was the baby of the family. Most of all she liked "Four" because she was "Four." In fact the girl liked "Four" so much that she secretly called her by a real name. When she was alone by the hutch, the girl would say, "Hello One! Hello Two! Hello Three!" to the first guinea pig babies. But when "Four" appeared, looking around to make sure that no one was near, the girl whispered, "Hello, Beryl!"

So of course Mom was right, and there was no point in getting fond of them. But by the end of the month the girl was very fond of the baby guinea pigs, especially of Beryl.

It had been agreed that the girl should go with Mom when she took the little pigs to the pet shop.

"I bet you'll cry," said the boy.

"I will not," said the girl. And she had really made up her mind that however sad she felt in the pet shop, she was not going to cry.

They took the guinea pigs to the pet shop in a basket and showed them to the pet shop man.

"Oh!" he said. "They *have* been well cared for."

And he got them out of the basket, One, Two, and Three.

"Just three, is it? They all seem fine, healthy specimens."

"No," said Mom, "there are four. There's another one down in the hay."

"So there is," said the man, lifting out Beryl. "She's not such a fine specimen as the others, is she?"

"She was born last," said Mom.

"That would account for it," said the man. But to the girl at that moment it seemed

"Oh!" he said. *"They* have
been well cared for."

perfectly obvious that Beryl was the most
beautiful guinea pig in the world.

"Well," said the man. "I don't know if I
can sell this last one—but for the other three,
I could give you one dollar each."

And the girl thought, "Oh *good*, I will be
able to keep Beryl after all."

But Mom said, "Please take all four. We
simply don't have room for the last one—if
you didn't like it, I'm afraid we should . . ."

The girl looked despondently at Mom.
What did she mean? There would be plenty
of room in the two hutches for just one extra
guinea pig.

"Oh, all right," said the man. "But I can
give you only fifty cents for the little one. She
is the runt of the litter."

The man put the little pigs into a cardboard
box and oh! how they squeaked. Seeing the
girl's face become anxious the man said, "I'm
just putting them in here until I've got the

window ready."

And then Mom and the girl went home, saying goodbye to the pigs in the shop. The girl had been very good and not cried. Walking home, the girl was also very good and didn't cry. But when she got home, she ran down to the hutches to talk to Tobacco and Hazel, and there she did cry—quietly, but for a long time.

Guinea pigs have shorter memories than we do. About ten minutes after the little pigs had gone to the pet shop, Tobacco called across from his cage to Hazel's, "Everything all right?"

And she replied, "Right you are."

"Kids all right?" he asked.

Now *kids*. Hazel knew there had been something on her mind. She had run into the living room to get them, and at that moment she had gotten distracted. A bowl of bread and milk had distracted her. And by the time she had eaten her fill, she had forgotten that she was looking for her children. Tobacco's question reminded her.

"Don't know where they've gone to," she called back.

"They'll be in the run—that's it," said Tobacco. "Out on the lawn."

By the time the girl came to commiserate with the grieving parents, both Hazel and Tobacco had more or less forgotten that they had ever *had* any children.

"Are you sad, darling Hazel?" asked the girl through her tears.

But Hazel called back politely, "Thank you for the bread and milk, ma'am. Very tasty."

"That's right," joined in Tobacco. "A very tasty piece of bread you gave me over here and all."

"Oh listen to how they are squeaking and missing their babies," said the girl.

Mom had come to join her.

"They'll be all right," said Mom. "They'll get over it."

"If you could ever manage to get us a *parsnip*," called Tobacco. "Now speaking for myself—I very much like parsnip."

"Oh it is sad," said Mom. "I think he really does miss the little ones."

The girl slept, but she woke very early the next morning. She knew as soon as she woke up that there was something to be sad about, but at first she could not remember what it was. And then the memory of yesterday returned with dreadful force, and she thought of the baby guinea pigs, squeaking in that box in the pet shop. She got up and put on her red flannel bathrobe and went downstairs and opened the back door. Outside in the garden the weather was sunny and cheerful. The birds were singing in the eaves of the house and in the forsythia bush. And somehow the fact that the world of nature looked and sounded so cheerful made the girl all the sadder. She went to the garden shed and opened the door.

"Sounds like breakfast," called Tobacco.

"Eh?" shouted Hazel from her hutch to his. "Breakfast, eh?"

"You *poor* things," said the girl when she heard their piping voices. But she had not brought their breakfast, which made them squeak all the more. So she opened Tobacco's hutch and took him back upstairs to her bedroom. She got back into bed and gave him a celery stick, which she had had the foresight to procure from the refrigerator on the way.

It was Saturday. The family had had their breakfast. Dad and the boy packed a basket and said that they were going out fishing. Mom said that she was going shopping, and when she had given the girl her allowance, the girl said she would like to go along with Mom. First they went to the grocer's and bought butter, cookies, cocoa, and cheese. Then they went to the butcher and bought a chicken and a pound of sausages. Then they went to the baker and bought fresh bread, four cupcakes, and two gingerbread men. And then they went to Mom's favorite café, and Mom had a cup of coffee, and the girl had a milk shake. Now all these stores and the café were in the covered market in the center of the town, in the very place where the pet shop was. It took the girl only two minutes to drink her milk shake through a straw, but Mom was lingering, in the annoying way that grown-ups linger over their drinks. She had hardly started her coffee.

"Mom," said the girl, "would it be all right if I went out and looked at a few store windows? I won't go far."

"Provided you don't leave the covered market," said Mom, "and provided you don't talk to strangers, and provided you are only five minutes."

So the girl left the café and walked to the next aisle of the market. And there on the corner was the pet shop window. There was a little group of people staring in at the window. Some were looking at a green lizard in a tank, and some were looking at the goldfish. But the greater part of them were looking at a lower window that contained . . . Beryl! There was Beryl, all on her own, nibbling some bran from a bowl and looking nonplussed by all this attention.

Evidently the other three babies had already been sold and, to judge from the talk at the window, Beryl would soon be sold too.

"Mom—get us a gerbil," said a little boy.

"You shut up," said his mother rudely.

Another mother was saying, "Isn't it sweet?"

"Can't we get it, Mommy, *please?*" said this other mother's daughter who looked—our girl considered—really horrible.

"Mom—get us a gerbil," said a little boy.
"You shut up," said his mother rudely.

Our girl had only planned to have one last look at her guinea pig babies. She only wanted to see them, and to say good-bye. She really had not planned what happened next, but she found herself looking in her purse. Mom had let her keep half the money from yesterday's transaction, so she had $1.75. In addition she had $.50 allowance from that morning and $1.00 in savings. Altogether she had $3.25. She had promised not to speak to strangers, but the man in the pet shop was not exactly a stranger. She found herself going into the shop. She felt very shy, and her heart was pounding excitedly.

The pet shop man took a long time before serving her. There were a lot of people in front of her, and every time they opened their mouths, the girl was afraid that they were going to ask if they could buy the guinea pig. But the man with the nobbly nose bought some dog food, and the short, fat woman with a scarf bought birdseed, and the two children bought hay . . . and at last it was the girl's turn.

"How much is the guinea pig in the window?" she blurted out shyly.

"At least you know what it is," laughed the man. "We had some people in just now who thought it was a gerbil. It's four dollars. Very fine guinea pig. It's been beautifully reared."

The man did not seem to recognize her as the girl who had sold him the guinea pigs the day before.

"You wouldn't take three dollars and twenty-five cents, I suppose," said the girl.

"Well," said the man. "The price is . . ." He peered at her. Did he know? "The price is really four dollars."

"It is rather a small, puny guinea pig," said the girl. "Do you have any others?"

"We had three others," said the man, "but they're all gone. Sold like hot cakes. And this," he paused, "this was the prize of the bunch." He was obviously weakening because he then said, "If you bought it, you would look after it properly, wouldn't you? It's been beautifully handled and reared since birth, this cavy."

"Oh, I would. I know how to look after guinea pigs. I have one or two already," said the girl.

"Three is the ideal number to have," said the man. "Two females and one male. This one here's a female."

The girl was clever. She did not say, "I know." She said instead, "You see, I only have three dollars and twenty-five cents. I could let you have the other seventy-five cents in a week." And then the man smiled and said, "Oh, all right. You can have it for three dollars and twenty-five cents."

A few minutes later the girl reappeared at the café, just as Mom was finishing her coffee.

She was carrying a little cardboard box, and out of it were coming the excited squeaks of Beryl.

"You don't need to tell me what you've got in there," Mom said. "I've guessed."

"I wasn't planning to buy her, really, Mom, I wasn't."

"Which one is it?" asked Mom. "I hope it *is* only one? Three guinea pigs is quite enough."

"It is Beryl," said the girl.

"Not One, Two, Three, or Four?"

"It is the one you call 'Four,' " said the girl.

"I won't call her 'Four' anymore," said Mom. "I will call her Beryl. Beryl is a good name."

About an hour later, Tobacco and Hazel were in their separate hutches.

"Coo-eee!"

"Is that you, girl?" asked Tobacco.

"No," said Hazel, "it wasn't me."

"Thought I heard you call. Nice celery this morning, mine was."

"I've tasted crisper," said Hazel, "but yes, it was nice."

"Coo-eee!"

"There you go again," said Tobacco.

"No I don't," said Hazel. "It's not me calling out. It's this new little brown 'un."

"Brown 'un?"

"Yes," said Hazel. "When they came around with the celery this morning, they put this new brown 'un in to share with me."

"Not a boar?" said Tobacco suspiciously. "You're not sharing your cage with no he-pig?"

"No, a little sow," said Hazel.

"That's all right then," said Tobacco. "Wonder why they didn't put her in to share with me?"

"She's nice," shouted Hazel. "More friendly to have someone to talk to."

"Not a boar?" said Tobacco suspiciously.
"No, a little sow," said Hazel.

"Coo-eee!" shouted Beryl.

"Funny idea, bringing in another," said Hazel, "when we were all right on our own. But friendly, certainly."

"Coo-eee, brown 'un!" shouted back Tobacco.

The

End